31 Inspirational

Whispers from the Unicorn

An Interactive journal with 31 inspirational quotes for young girls and women

By Felicia Starshine

ISBN 13: 978-1790953004

Acknowledgements

Our heartfelt gratitude to:

Edward Andes, George Ndwiga and Kevin Kibiego;
for their invaluable contribution in making
this magical journal come alive.

Serajus Salehin; for his excellent ideas
and extraordinary designing.

Tet Cuales; for blessing every page
with a unique unicorn sparkle.

Purpose of this journal

Be empowered. Felicia Starshine, the Queen of all Unicorns, empowers you to become more in tune with your goals and aspirations. Her daily whispers are an inspiration to young girls and women all around the world.

Unlimited possibilities. Felicia Starshine envisions a world where the dreams you dare to dream really do come true. The Unicorn Queen wants you therefore to dream big and imagine a life of unlimited possibilities.

Touch and inspire others. Felicia Starshine's 31-day inspirational quotes journal aims to bring out the best in you so you can touch and inspire others and help them to make their dreams a reality as well.

Be interactive and understand who you really are. Felicia Starshine, the Queen of all Unicorns, empowers you to not just believe in your dreams but to also move forward in making those dreams a reality. She therefore invited you to reflect and get to know yourself better with this well-designed 31-day Inspirational and Interactive Quotes Journal. Answer the questions at the end of every daily whisper and you will find yourself more inspired and in tune with your inner self than ever.

Get ready for some
unicorn magic!

There is nothing more powerful

Than a *Passionate Individual*

With a Dream

TO CHANGE THE WORLD

Write down your 3 most audacious dreams.

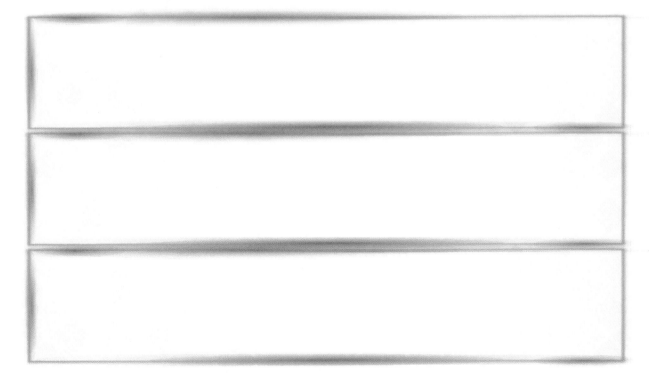

Have a **WHY** to live and you will be able to bear with almost any **HOW**

List 5 reasons why you want to realise your dreams.

★

★

★

★

★

Imagine
with all your mind
Believe
with all your heart
Act
with all your potential

What is easiest for you: Imagining your goal? Believing it? or Acting on it? Please explain why.

We unicorns believe that there is magic in trying to do The impossible

List 1 thing that may seem impossible to achieve and write down what you would have to do to make it happen.

With **IMAGINATION** & *Faith* Magic *Starts to happen*

What are 3 goals you want to achieve in 1 year time?

When you hear a whisper

listen carefully

it's the Unicorns

playing in the sky

Write down three things that make your heart beat faster.

-
-
-

Believe

In yourself

And

You will soon

find yourself doing

unbelievable things

List three things that you can do today that will bring you a step closer to reaching your dreams.

-
-
-

When life hits you
Get up!
When life hits you again
get up again!
Do not give up
Ever

Describe a short event where you were thinking to give up and then you didn't. How did that make you feel?

It's not

The size of the unicorn

in the dream

it's the size of the dream

in the

Unicorn

List three big dreams you would like to accomplish in 10 years time.

-
-
-

"Never doubt that you are

Valuable
Powerful
Deserving
"

Write down 3 things that make you valuable.

3 things that make you powerful.

3 things that make you deserving.

Embrace
Your uniqueness

Stay True
To You

Believe In Miracles

Sparkle

From within

Write down 5 personal traits that make you unique.

When you feel
Alone & Lost
Trust Your
Unicorn Heart
&
Keep Moving

FORWARD

List 5 things you can be immensely grateful for.

Those Who Don't Believe In Magic Will Never ★ Find It ★

Write down an instance wherein you had a hard time achieving a goal.
What did you do and what would you do differently today?

All it takes is

Faith & Trust

and a little

Unicorn Dust

If you had my unicorn powers and you could make instant changes, what 3 things would you change about your life and why?

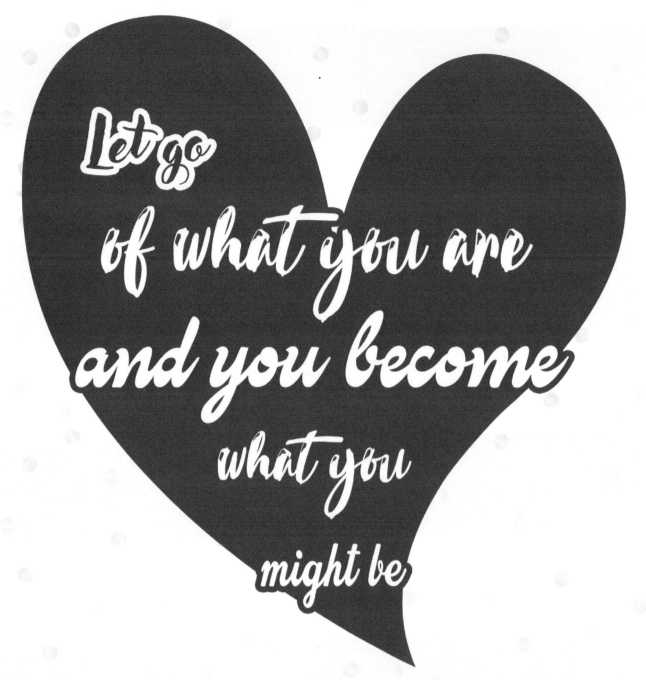

Let go of what you are and you become what you might be

List 3 limiting beliefs that are preventing you from realizing your dream and what could you do to overcome them?

" Prepare
and one day your
Chance
will come "

List 3 successes that have brought you closer to the realisation of your dreams.

List 3 things that you will accomplish during the next 30 days.

Be passionate
like a Unicorn
because when things get hard
Your Passion
will pull you through

Write down 5 things you are passionate about.

Don't think for a second that you are too young or *too old* to have big dreams

What are your seven main aspirations for the next 18 months?

-
-
-
-
-
-
-

When someone tells you that
You can't
turn around and say
Watch me

List 3 persons in your life that you feel are negative and dragging you down.

-
-
-

List 3 persons that inspire you and push you forward.

-
-
-

How could you make sure to spend more time with the second group?

A Unicorn never puts a limit on anything *because the more* we dream *the* Further we get

If you had total freedom to aspire anything without having to take into account potential obstacles, what would be your top 5 aspirations?

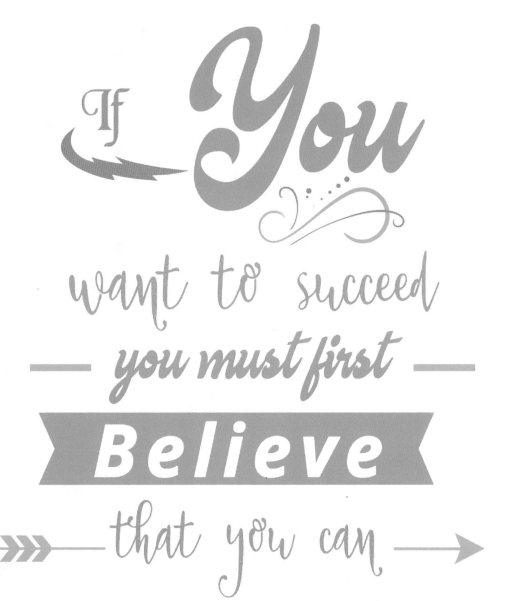

If **You** want to succeed — you must first — **Believe** — that you can →

List 5 of your main fears and write next to each what you could do to start overcoming them.

Unicorns live their lives as if everything was a Miracle

Think about one specific situation in your life that felt like a miracle to you and write it down. How did you feel?

Failure

does not exist

it is merely

an experiment

on the path

to

Success

Please write down 3 instances where you were able to overcome a tough challenge.

-
-
-

Being perfect

won't make you move mountains

IMAGINATION will

List 3 things on which you spend too much time.

-
-
-

3 things on which you don't spend enough time.

-
-
-

Now imagine how you could shift your focus to the things that really matter.

Nothing makes a

Unicorn

more happy than

People

who follow

Their Dreams

List 5 things for which you are very happy today.

Every girl in this world

Is beautiful in her own way

And that is what

Makes the world beautiful

List 5 things that make you a beautiful human being.

★

★

★

★

★

Make Your Life a MASTERPIECE

What does your masterpiece life look like?

The magic secret of us, *Unicorns* is that we are *Fearless* in the pursuit of what sets our *Soul on fire*

List your top 3 fears. Write down how you could overcome them.

-
-
-

If you stay in your comfort zone

you may experience motion and confuse it with action

If you get out of your comfort zone

you will make real progress

without confusing it with anything else

List 3 things you have always wanted to try and write down the reasons why you haven't done them. Then write down what you would have to do to make them happen.

> Let your dreams
> be the Stars
> &
> your Dedication
> the Rocket Ship

List 5 commitments you are going to make this week

(they can be small or big) and stick to them.

-
-
-
-
-

The real question

comes down to this

Do you have what it takes

to be a Unicorn?

Do you have what it takes to pursue your dreams and why do you believe that?

Felicia Starshine says that we have to embrace our uniqueness, stay true to ourselves, believe in miracles and sparkle from within. She envisions a world where the dreams you dare to dream really do come true. She also believes that it i fundamental in life to develop your imagination, to believe in yourself and to follow your dreams. This is the essence what she stands for. Spreading this message with the world is the ultimate purpose of our brand.

Felicia Starshine was born in a land far, far away where rainbows never ended where rainstorms came down as glitter, where the mountains were soft like cotto wool and where everything was painted in color. Felicia was born among unicorn and even now until this day, she visits her much loved friends and sometimes eve takes a ride to the moon with them.

Felicia learned to treasure the good things in life and cherish the small moments tha made her happy. To fill the children of this world with joy, she wrote this interactiv journal and sees it as a way to give back just a little piece of magic, just as th unicorns gave to her.

"Believe in yourself and you will soon find yourself doing unbelievable things." - Felicia Starshine

Felicia St★rshine

Printed in Great Britain
by Amazon